Creating our Eden

by
Jaylene Rodriguez-Garau

Edited by Anna Roberts
Cover and Interior Design by Cactus Rose Designs

A Note from the Author

Hello and thank you so much for picking up this book! I'm not sure where you are on your faith journey, but wherever you are, I'm so glad and grateful that you're here reading this! My hope is that you will not only enjoy this story but also feel inspired to put God first in your life. If you're already doing that, that's amazing—please join me in sharing this message with others!

Since I was a child, I believed in God, but I didn't realize that I could have a personal relationship with Him. It wasn't until I was almost forty that I made the decision to put God first in my life, and it changed everything! That's why I write: to encourage others to seek God and discover the beauty of truly knowing Him.

All the best,
Jaylene

P.S. I'd love to hear from you! Come say hi over at www.jaylenerodriguezgarau.com.

Chapter One

"In this world you will have trouble. But take heart! I have overcome the world." John 16:33

SHE KICKED OFF HER black stilettos and raced toward the fire. Her long evening gown thrashed behind her as she dashed across the lawn toward her house. Nothing would stand in her way.

"Stop!" yelled a voice.

Becky Ruiz would normally stop for a police officer's command, but not today. There was too much at stake. She had to tell the firefighters her dog was inside. She screamed, but the noise of the fire trucks and the rushing water drowned out her cries.

Suddenly she felt a grab at her arm. The officer pleaded with her to come with him. Becky pulled away. "I have to get my dog out!"

"A neighbor has your dog!" shouted the officer over the engines' humming. He motioned to look behind her.

Everything grew silent as relief washed over Becky when she saw those unmistakable brown eyes looking back at her. She scooped Alma into her arms and held the small, shivering dog close to her body. She stroked her black fur to comfort her. *Alma* means soul in Spanish, and Becky felt her soul needed soothing as much as the dog did. She was so grateful the firefighters rescued her.

Becky went from numbness to wanting to scream out to the firefighters to save her home, but it was hopeless. It was clear the fire had the upper hand. Becky's beautiful two-story suburban home tucked away in a quiet Florida cul-de-sac was an inferno, and there was nothing anyone could do to salvage it. Every window of her home gushed with bright flames. As the fire raged, Becky gave up hope that anything would be spared. The firefighters' efforts were dwarfed by the magnitude of the fire.

"The house is fully involved." Becky heard a voice come through a nearby walkie-talkie. She stood transfixed, staring at her house where she had raised her two children, who were now away at college. She saw flashes of memories. The kids running down the stairs on Christmas morning, first day of school photos taken on the porch, family dinners around the table, and s'mores by the fireplace. The cruel irony of always keeping a home immaculate to have it reduced to rubble.

The sky on this chilly December night was filled with ash floating everywhere. Some made their way toward Becky, almost as if to say goodbye. She reached out to touch them, hoping to touch remnants of her home and her belongings one last time. It was hard to stand and watch, but she could not leave. She felt she owed it to her home of nearly twenty years to be there in its demise.

The scene was so loud. The hum of the fire trucks, the water from the hoses dousing the flames, and the chattering of the neighbors who had gathered. It was dark except for the flashes of red lights from the emergency vehicles. It all felt surreal to Becky. She went inward. It was the only place where it was quiet.

Her husband, Mark, came from behind and draped her with a black shawl she had left in the car. They had rushed home from Mark's company holiday party after a neighbor called to tell them about the fire. Becky immediately felt her body comforted by the warm cashmere shawl and by Mark's steadfast presence. He tried to persuade her to come with him, to look away, but she could not. So he stayed with her.

"How are we going to tell the kids, Mark?"

Mark didn't have an answer. He held Becky close.

The solemn moment was interrupted by their neighbor, Mr. Samuel. He raced toward them, clearly agitated. "I saw a man wearing a black jacket with a hood pulled over his head running from the side of your house just before I noticed your house was on fire!"

Chapter Two

> "The Lord is close to the brokenhearted and
> saves those who are crushed in spirit."
> Psalm 34:18

DESPITE THE FIREFIGHTERS' EFFORTS, the Ruiz home was a total loss. Becky and Mark spent the night at a hotel. Alma stayed with a neighbor. All they possessed was their car, borrowed clothes from neighbors, and a handful of toiletries they hastily picked up at a drugstore.

Losing her dream home was hard, but what was lost inside left Becky gutted. The Mother's Day handprint cards that her kids made in preschool, her wedding album, and the cross necklace her mother wore every day before she passed away. Those were just a few of the many keepsakes that were likely lost. Items that could never be replaced.

Becky reeked of fire. The burnt scent was infused in her clothes and in every strand of her thick, wavy hair, hauntingly reminding her of all it took.

She went in the shower. She wanted to scrub the stench away. She let the water run down her, yearning to wash away the smell in her hair and the sorrow in her heart. She sobbed from deep within. A sob of despair reverberated in every part of her. Her mind wandered to so many questions she was making herself sick. Her head was pounding, and her stomach was in knots. They didn't have a house for her children to come home to. That was the most agonizing of all for Becky.

Chapter Three

"Blessed are those who mourn, for they will be comforted." Matthew 5:4

WHEN BECKY WOKE UP in the hotel the following day, still groggy, it took her a few seconds to get her bearings and remember why she was there. When the reality hit, it ached to be reacquainted with her loss. She wanted to close her eyes again, wishing sleep would give her an escape from the grief. She felt defeated. She had so much to do, but she couldn't muster up the energy to get out of bed.

She thought of all the calls she had to make. She needed to call the office and tell them she couldn't make it to the mediation. Becky prided herself on always being dependable. She was known as a workhorse at the law firm, but she knew she wasn't in the right mindset to represent her client well. She also needed to find a hotel that allowed dogs, or plan for Alma to stay with the neighbor longer. She had to call the insurance company and follow up with the fire department.

Then the thought she was avoiding came rushing in and pushed every other thought aside. Her mind grew silent, and she wept. Becky thought of her neighbor who saw someone run from her house the night of the fire. Although investigators spoke to Becky and Mark that night, neither of them had any idea who that person could be.

Why would someone want to set our house on fire?

Before Becky could finish her thought, Mark walked into the room with a cup of coffee and a croissant. "Good, you're up!" Mark said enthusiastically, balancing the cup and plate in his hands while holding his leg out so the heavy door wouldn't slam behind him. "They had quite a breakfast selection in the lobby."

Typical Mark, Becky thought. Their world had fallen apart, and here he was making small talk. *Does he not get the enormity of this? What we've lost! Someone who hates us is still out there. What if the person thought we were home and meant to kill us, and now they want to finish us off?*

Becky knew not to voice those thoughts to Mark. He often shrugged off her concerns. Sure, she could sometimes be paranoid and think of worst-case scenarios. She attributed it to having an attorney's mind who was prone to anxiety, but Mark often dismissed her concerns even when they were valid. It frustrated her, especially because this was a worst-case scenario!

"Mark, there are so many calls I need to make." Becky got out of bed and put the cup of coffee that Mark had just handed her on the nightstand.

"I've got it. Just relax." Mark picked up her phone from the nightstand and put it behind his back. "Why don't you go have lunch with Harper today? It will make you feel better."

Mark was right; time with her best friend was what she needed, but Becky didn't know how to feel about Mark taking everything off her plate.

"You have to go out to lunch today. How can you miss out on wearing this beauty?" Mark laughed as he poked out from behind a ladies' coat held out in front of him.

Becky smiled when she saw Mrs. Gibbons's coat. Their eighty-five-year-old next-door neighbor, Mrs. Gibbons, was one of the kindest women Becky had ever known. When the kids were little, she had often watched Katie and Josh for Becky and Mark.

Mrs. Gibbons did all she could to comfort Becky and Mark the night of the fire. She brought over her homemade pound cake and bags of clothes for Becky to borrow, including her signature lavender wool coat that Mark was holding. It had an oversized collar embellished with pearls. It wasn't Becky's style, but she was grateful for the gesture. So many of her neighbors had helped in any way they could.

"You'll look so distinguished in this."

Becky took the coat from Mark and held it. The unmistakable scent of Jean Nate perfume tickled her nose. "Aw, Mrs. Gibbons." She pulled the coat toward her chest and dug her nose into the collar. The sweet scent of her kindhearted neighbor comforted her. It reminded her of home.

Chapter Four

"As iron sharpens iron, so one person sharpens another." Proverbs 27:17

CLOAKED IN MRS. GIBBONS'S lavender coat, Becky made her way to meet Harper. They would meet at their regular place. Nestled in their ever-growing suburb, was a small historic downtown lined with quaint shops and restaurants tucked under expansive oak trees. Becky and Harper prided themselves on having visited most of those places together. Once a week throughout their thirty-year friendship, they met for coffee, lunch, or shopping. They had started when they were in college and continued while living in Winter Garden and raising their kids.

Becky and Harper had experienced many of the same milestones together. They became first-time moms within months of each other, and most recently, they became empty nesters. They had shared many personal highs and lows through the years. This was a low Becky could never have imagined or prepared for.

As Becky crossed the brick-paved street, she spotted Harper seated at a small table on the sidewalk. Glistening in the sun was her glossy, straight black hair cropped right at her shoulders. Her petite frame sat very upright while she read the menu. As soon as Becky caught sight of Harper, it was as if Harper felt Becky's presence, and she immediately looked up. When friends connect as deeply and as long as Becky and Harper had, one can sense when the other is near.

Harper stood up and quickly walked toward Becky to embrace her. The moment Becky felt Harper's arms wrap around her, she felt the tension in her body melt away. Becky broke down in tears. She could finally let go. Harper had heard about the fire, and there was so much Becky had to catch her up on, but at that moment, all Becky wanted to do was take in that secure embrace from her best friend.

The two eventually sat down. Harper always found the right words to say, but it was hard to find the right words for this, so she just listened while she held Becky's hand across the table.

"It feels surreal," Becky let out through her tears. "We lost everything. We had planned things so meticulously. Mark worked long hours at the architecture firm. I took on more cases for extra income. We sacrificed time with the kids to get ahead, and for what? In one night, we lost everything that we worked a lifetime for." Becky fumed. "We did everything right, Harper. Why us? Why our home? It just feels so unfair!"

Becky's parents had immigrated from Cuba in the 1960s, fleeing communism. When they arrived in the United States, they owned only the clothes on their backs. For as long as Becky could remember, she was determined to make their sacrifice worthwhile. She chased hard after the American dream, she attained it, and now most of it was gone.

"The irony of having my parents come to this country owning only the clothes on their backs, and now decades later, here I am in the same situation!" Frustrated, she grabbed the sleeve of the wool jacket she was wearing. "I don't even own this jacket." That realization stung. Tears streamed down, and suddenly laughter erupted. "I don't even own this jacket." Becky laughed nervously at the irony. "Sometimes you have to laugh so you don't fall apart completely."

Taking a cue from Becky, Harper began to laugh too. Harper's face was sopping wet from her own tears. Harper was the kind of person who bears a friend's burdens. She held Becky's hand tighter as she looked into her eyes. They both smiled at each other.

The exchange was interrupted by a familiar Christmas carol playing nearby. Every year, downtown Winter Garden was decked out for Christmas. People scurried around shopping for the holidays. Becky felt bitter as she watched people walk by with bags in hand and holiday-themed coffee cups. Her life had fallen apart, but life continued all around her. She didn't have a house to decorate. She didn't even have her own home to sleep in. That reality was painful.

Becky longed to sit in the quiet den of her home with her feet up near the fireplace, reading a book. She would miss the season's traditions, like baking cookies with her son and decorating the tree with the kids. Even though they were older, they still enjoyed those traditions. When Becky and Mark had broken the news about the fire to the kids, they promised them that they would rebuild. They hoped that by next Christmas, they would be in their newly built home.

"I'm so sorry this is happening to you," Harper said. "You and Mark can stay with us as long you need to."

Harper had barely finished the sentence when Becky interrupted. "I can't." Becky was usually the first to help others, but it was hard for her to accept help.

"I was hoping you'd take me up on my offer, but I know you," Harper said. "So here's something to think about. Jake found out about the fire.

He contacted me and asked if you and Mark would like to stay in a cottage he owns in Tennessee. It's one of his vacation homes."

Becky didn't hear anything past the name Jake. Feelings of animosity swelled inside of her.

"Becky?" Harper reached out to hold her other hand. "Becky?" Harper tried to get her attention. "Jake wants to put the cottage on the market next summer. He says you can stay there for free until you figure things out. The cottage is updated. It just needs a little TLC." Harper believed that going to Tennessee and having a project to work on would help Becky, so she did not let up. "The cottage is on a large piece of land in the countryside. The land needs some tending to, but with your green thumb, it will be great."

Becky didn't say a word. Harper paused to catch her breath.

Becky pulled her hands away from Harper. "Of course Jake would offer to help with a caveat: to help himself! He needs someone to fix the place up, so why not get free labor from poor Becky and Mark, who are desperate because they don't have a roof over their heads? Typical Jake!"

"Becky, you'll never even have to see Jake. He lives in Miami, and I hear that he hasn't been to the cottage in a few years. You'll only deal with a management company."

Becky was still reluctant. "I'll talk to Mark about it." Becky wasn't sure if she said she would talk to Mark because she would mention it to him, or because she just wanted Harper to stop talking about Jake.

Chapter Five

"Forget the former things; do not dwell on the past. See, I am doing a new thing!"
Isaiah 43:18-19

WHEN BECKY ARRIVED AT the hotel, she found Mark working at the small desk in the cramped room.

"Hey, Becky, I couldn't find a hotel nearby that allows dogs. Do you want to try looking? Maybe you'll have better luck finding one."

Becky wanted to say that she would look for a hotel online that night, but instead, she told Mark about the offer to stay in Jake's cottage. There was a part of Becky that wanted to stay in Winter Garden. It was home and she loved to be near her friends, but other times, she just wanted to run away from the mess that had become her life and return when her new house was built.

"Maybe going up to Tennessee will be good for us, Mark. I've taken leave from work, and Alma will have plenty of space to run." Becky looked hopeful for the first time since the fire.

Mark was hesitant to deal with Jake again. It had been decades since he had last seen him. That last meeting ended horribly, but after seeing Becky hopeful, he wanted to please her.

"I'll call Greg and see if I can work remotely," Mark said.

Within minutes, Mark got off the phone with his boss. "Greg said yes. We can go."

Instead of joy, Becky and Mark felt trepidation. They were headed to a place owned by a man neither of them trusted, but the fire left them with few choices. They chose what landed on their laps because it was easier than looking for a rental, and they hoped the change of scenery would lift their spirits.

Chapter Six

"Trust in the Lord with all your heart and lean not on your own understanding." Proverbs 3:5

"THIS IS THE EASIEST trip we've ever packed for." Mark tried to lighten the mood. "Everything we own fits in one borrowed suitcase."

Mark and Becky headed out on the ten-hour drive to Tennessee with Alma in tow. Having Alma back with them brought a sense of some normalcy.

"What's the name of the town we're going to, anyway?" Mark asked.

"It's not a town; it's considered a rural village," Becky answered as she typed an address in the car's GPS.

Nearly ten hours later, Mark and Becky arrived in the village. They needed to meet up with a man named Hank from the property management company to get the key for the cottage. As they scanned the narrow main road of the town looking for the company, they could not find a sign for it on any of the buildings.

"That's odd. Are you sure you typed in the right address?" Mark asked as he slowed the car down.

"That's it, over there!" Becky pointed to a small general store called H & H.

Becky and Mark thought it was odd the address led them to general store, but they went in and asked for Hank. Hank ran the property management company out of the general store that he and his wife, Hilda, owned. It was a one-stop shop.

"How are y'all doing?" asked Hank. His enthusiasm made Becky and Mark feel immediately welcomed.

Hilda peered from behind the coffee counter. "Hi, I'm Hilda; you must be Mr. and Mrs. Ruiz!"

"Oh, you can call us Becky and Mark." Becky wondered how Hilda knew who they were just by looking at them.

"Well, you two are in for quite a treat. The cottage is a real beauty! It was featured in *Southern Living* magazine right before Jake bought it."

Becky reached for the key and thought, *Of course Jake would buy a cottage featured in a magazine. He's always been about image and getting the next "best" thing.*

"Should we tell them about the hidden treasure on the property?" Hilda asked in a mysterious whisper directed at Hank but loud enough for Becky and Mark to overhear.

Becky and Mark were so exhausted from the drive that they didn't bite, so Hank took the bait. Hank and Hilda were like a two-person play, taking cues from each other.

"Oh yes, the treasure!" Hank opened his eyes wide. "The cottage was built in the 1960s by Joseph Carter. He hit it big as a music producer in Nashville, but when he died, he didn't have a cent to his name, so it's rumored that he buried his entire fortune on that land."

Hank and Hilda waited for some response from Becky and Mark. Becky and Mark didn't want to be rude, but they just wanted to get to the cottage after the long drive.

"I put some fresh sheets and towels in the cottage for you," Hilda said. "Let us know if you need anything. Your closest neighbor is Mrs. Melody. She owns the Rose Garden Bed and Breakfast. She can also help with anything you need. She knows y'all are coming."

With that, Becky and Mark thanked Hank and Hilda and parted ways.

"They really couldn't be more welcoming," Becky said as they left the general store.

"Yeah, but they were a bit *too* welcoming. It was awkward."

"It's Southern hospitality, Mark. We're the awkward ones."

Chapter Seven

"Now faith is confidence in what we hope for and assurance about what we do not see."
Hebrews 11:1

TWENTY MINUTES AND SEVERAL winding roads later, there in the distance, they saw the cottage. It was dusk, so it was hard to make out the number on the post.

"Do you think this is it?" Becky asked, even though the GPS showed that exact location.

Mark turned into the long driveway that cut through the heavily wooded property and right to the cottage.

"It's so pretty! It looks like a cottage out of a storybook." Becky was eager to go inside. She flung the car door open, and Alma jumped out behind her.

As Alma neared the side of the cottage, she suddenly stopped short and growled.

"What is it, Alma?" Mark came closer. He felt slightly on edge because it was too dark to see what Alma was fussing about. He turned on the flashlight on his phone and pointed it in the direction Alma was focused on. Immediately he noticed a set of eyes looking back at him. "Oh, it's just a possum!" he called out.

"Come on, Alma!" Becky called as she unlocked the front door of the cottage and stepped in. "I'm not sure what to think."

Mark followed behind. "Yeah, it's interesting."

The cottage had been updated, but the inside didn't match the outside. There was no charm. It was sterile. Becky had a knack for decorating and began envisioning what she could do to make it more welcoming. Jake had provided a prepaid card for expenses related to the cottage.

Becky walked over to the kitchen and found a note. It was from Hilda and Hank.

Dear Mr. and Mrs. Ruiz,

We took the liberty of stocking the fridge and pantry with a few items from our store to get you through the first few days.

Enjoy,

Hilda and Hank

"That was nice," Becky said, calling Mark over to show him the note. "You see, it's just Southern hospitality."

Chapter Eight

"And now these three remain: faith, hope and love. But the greatest of these is love."
1 Corinthians 13:13

BECKY AND MARK HAD hoped to sleep in, but the windows didn't have curtains, so they woke up when the sun came up.

Mark stumbled into the kitchen to make coffee. Later, Becky joined him. They sat near a window overlooking a clearing in the woods. Suddenly deer began to appear until there was a small herd gathered. Becky and Mark were captivated. A mountainous terrain was a special treat for them because it was so different from Florida, but seeing this herd of deer made it extra special.

It was rare for Becky and Mark to sit together for coffee anymore. Early on in their marriage, they had "coffee talk" every morning in their small apartment, and they would dream together. They talked about their career goals, trips they wanted to take together, and wondered about the kids they would have one day. Becky could not remember when, but sometime along the way, their coffee talks stopped. Becky and Mark, who were once each other's best friends, drifted apart.

Their marriage took the backseat to raising their children. As the kids got older, their schedules became busier. Mark and Becky juggled their careers while shuttling the kids to a daily deluge of activities. They didn't carve out time to connect as husband and wife; everything else was a priority. Once the kids left for college, they felt like strangers to one another. Becky wondered if Mark had fallen out of love with her. Mark wondered the same about Becky.

"So where do we start?" asked Mark, hoping to get busy on a to-do list for the cottage.

"Well, we know what needs to get done inside, but we haven't taken a look outside, so maybe we can start there today," Becky said as she put on a jacket.

Keeping busy is how Becky and Mark dealt with the problems in their marriage. They seemed unaware that even small grievances, if left unaddressed over time, can chip away and claim a marriage.

Chapter Nine

"I lift up my eyes to the mountains—where does my help come from?" Psalm 121:1

OVERWHELMED IS HOW BECKY and Mark felt after surveying the land—seven acres of overgrown vegetation and empty garden beds. Thankfully, it was a mild winter, so Becky and Mark could at least begin clearing the brush.

"I think we've bitten off more than we can chew," said Becky, holding her forehead.

"It will take time, but time is the one thing we have." Mark stretched his arms out. "Look at all of this. We have a lot to help keep our minds off our troubles."

"Speaking of trouble, who is that coming onto the property?" Becky motioned to Mark to look behind him.

The person was so far away that Becky and Mark could not make out any details. One thing was clear: The person was headed straight in their direction with a determined stride. It made Becky a little nervous.

"I hope we're not already making enemies out here. In these small villages, locals can be wary of outsiders' motives." Becky's mind often spun worrisome scenarios.

As the person got closer, Mark and Becky noticed it was an older woman. She gave a friendly wave that put Becky at ease. The woman appeared very poised. She was quite spry for someone her age. Most of her gray hair was tucked under a straw hat draped with a white silk bow. A German shepherd walked alongside her, running off every few steps to frolic in the tall grass and then returning to the woman's side.

"Hi, I'm Mrs. Melody!" the woman called out, hoping to put Becky and Mark's curiosity to rest. "I'm your next-door neighbor," she said as she got closer. She was a little out of breath. "Well, next-door is relative; these properties are quite large." She laughed joyfully.

"It's so nice to meet you, Mrs. Melody," Mark said, stretching out his hand.

Becky reached out to shake Mrs. Melody's hand as well. "Hilda from the general store told us about you."

Mrs. Melody placed the basket she was carrying on the ground. "Come here, kids," she said, opening her arms wide. Her hands motioned to Becky and Mark to come in for a hug.

Mark and Becky briefly looked at each other, a little taken aback; they were not accustomed to such warm hospitality from a stranger. They went in for the hug together. Mrs. Melody opened her arms wide to accommodate the two of them.

"Hilda told me about the fire, and I'm so sorry that happened to y'all. Come, I have something for you."

Mrs. Melody carried herself with confidence, but she also had a softness to her. She walked Becky and Mark to a small table on the cottage's back porch. Mrs. Melody unveiled what she had in her basket. It was a pie. She cut into it and gave Becky and Mark each a slice on the floral melamine plates she had brought.

Mark dug into his slice. "Mm . . . this is good."

"Thank you. It's my mom's recipe. She used to cook for a wealthy family in town when I was a child. Everyone loved her cookin'."

Becky's eyes closed as she savored it. "I think this is the best pie I've ever eaten!"

"I'm glad," said Mrs. Melody. "Hope it's not too sweet."

"No, it's perfect."

"Does it taste a little bitter?"

Becky paused to take another bite. She chewed pensively. "Come to think of it, it does taste a little bitter."

Immediately after saying that, Becky wanted to take it back. "I'm so sorry; I didn't mean to say it's bitter. I mean, somehow, the sweetness and the bitterness work together. It's so good."

Mrs. Melody laughed. "You didn't offend me, honey. I hope it's a little bitter. It's called bittersweet chocolate pie. My mama used to say our lives are like bittersweet pie . . . a little bitter and a little sweet. It's the combination that makes it distinctly good. So how long will y'all be here?"

"We're not sure."

"This sweet cottage needs a little lovin'. Hope y'all stay awhile."

"Looking at all that needs to get done around here, I think we'll be here for longer than we thought," said Becky.

"I'm happy to hear that!" Mrs. Melody stood up from the chair. "I'll let you kids get back to what you were doing. Enjoy the rest of the pie."

"How do we get this container back to you?" asked Becky. The ornate container looked vintage and made of glass.

"Oh, just come to my house to drop it off. There's a river further back. Walk alongside it, and it will lead you to the back of my house."

Becky preferred more detailed directions. "May I have your address, please? I'll just drive over. It may be easier, since I don't know my way around yet."

"If you drive, you'll miss out on so much. Follow the bank of the river, and I promise you won't get lost. The only GPS we use around these parts is God's Positioning System."

Chapter Ten

"Be still, and know that I am God." Psalm 46:10

ALTHOUGH IT HAD ONLY been a short time, Becky found work at the cottage fulfilling. It kept her mind occupied and off of all she lost. The work was also different than work back at home. Balancing the demands at the law firm and managing her large home made for a frenzied life. Here, with fewer demands, she had more time to be truly present, and she returned to writing, one of her favorite pastimes. It seemed there was more inspiration here. The glorious sunset that cast a warm glow on the landscape every evening and the many wildlife sightings left Becky in awe. Beauty was all around her back at home too, but she rarely noticed. Becky felt so alive now. Despite the abundance of life surrounding her, one thing still felt dead—her marriage.

Becky wished she could just meet up for coffee with Harper. She felt so isolated. Although Becky and Harper spoke on the phone frequently, Becky longed to see her friend in person. Since there was no chance of seeing Harper anytime soon, Becky decided to write a letter to her. Writing usually made Becky feel better.

January 10, 2023

Dear Harper,

I hope you're well. There's so much I need to catch you up on! I know it's odd to write a letter to you rather than call, but I thought I'd write to you like we did when we were apart that summer in college. Besides, you know how much I love to write!

We continue to enjoy Tennessee! We discovered a great lunch spot in the village last week. Some parts of the town remind me of our downtown. So charming. The people here have made us feel welcomed! It's true what they say about Southern hospitality. When we spoke last, I forgot to mention that we met one of our neighbors. Her name is Mrs. Melody. She's kind and also a no-nonsense kind of woman. When I grow up, I hope to be like Mrs. Melody. LOL

As you know, the kids came for Christmas. The cottage only has two bedrooms and one bathroom, so we were pretty cramped. Katie slept in the spare room. It's less than half the size of her room at our old house. Josh slept on the couch. As you can imagine, they weren't too happy about it. Oh well. We've all had to adjust. On the bright side, because the cottage is so small, it's much quicker to clean than our old house. The internet is spotty out here, so with less time on electronics, we've spent much more time together as a family, which has been nice.

The cottage felt especially quiet once the kids left after the New Year. Mark and I are still having the same issues. We just don't connect like we once did. We're either really short with each other or we barely have anything to talk about beyond small talk. I miss us.

Mark did do something really sweet for me recently. He built a garden bed for me! You know I always wanted to start a vegetable garden at home, but we never had the time to start one, let alone the time to tend to one.

Remember the adorable greenhouse I told you about the last time we chatted on the phone? We're growing vegetable plants in there for now until it warms up, and then we'll plant them in the ground. I spend a lot of time in the greenhouse tending to the plants. I love being in there! You were right; this place has been wonderful for me in many ways.

Last time we were on the phone, I didn't get to update you on the fire investigation. They're saying it started in the closet of our master bedroom where we had the safe. The safe didn't burn because it's fireproof. They believe it was arson and likely robbery. We still don't have a clue as to who could have done this! I want to know, and sometimes I just want to stay in the greenhouse tending to the plants and not think about any of this.

As for the house, there's not much to update. We're still waiting on insurance and contractors.

On a happier note, let me know what's new with you. How's Melinda adjusting to the new semester at school? I miss you, Harper!

Love you,

Becky

Chapter Eleven

"For where your treasure is, there your heart will be also." Matthew 6:21

MARK HAD BOUGHT QUITE a variety of vegetable plants from the local nursery. As a thank-you for the purchase, Mack, the nursery owner, had three small trees delivered to the cottage. Mark hadn't gotten around to planting the trees yet. He wanted Becky's input as to where to plant them.

"That was nice of Mack to have these trees sent over," Becky said as she looked over the tags to see what kind of trees they were. "Mm . . . apple, peach, and fig."

Mark grabbed the shovel. "The trees are young; it will be years before they bear fruit."

"Yeah, we'll be back home well before then, but someone will enjoy them."

After Mark and Becky decided where to plant the trees, Mark began digging. For each tree, Mark placed it in the hole and Becky held it steady while Mark packed soil all around it.

When they went to plant the final tree, the fig tree, Mark felt the hole needed to be a little deeper. As he was digging, he hit something. He dug at it with the shovel, thinking it was a root, but it wasn't giving way. He grabbed at it with his hand. It wasn't a root. It was a metal box.

"What is it, Mark?"

"I'm not sure." Mark handed the box to Becky. "Do you think it's that treasure of fortunes that Hank and Hilda told us about?" He laughed because the box was so small.

Becky shook the box. "Well, if it's a fortune, it's a small one."

When Becky opened the box, she found a Bible inside. It appeared old. The leather cover was tattered.

"Maybe there's money tucked away in the pages," Mark said as he peered over.

Becky opened the Bible and flipped through the pages. She found a black-and-white photo tucked away between two pages. On the back, someone had written names, ages, and the year the photo was taken. It appeared to be a family, and they were standing in front of the cottage.

Joseph Carter, 30

Elizabeth Carter, 28

Emma Carter, newborn

1965

"Joseph Carter . . . isn't that the guy Hank told us about who built the cottage?" Becky handed the photo to Mark.

"Yeah, the one who made it big as a music producer in Nashville," Mark recalled. "So there's nothing else tucked in the pages?"

"No, I guess that's it." Becky carefully tucked the photo into the Bible.

Mark and Becky went back to planting the fig tree. Becky held the tree in place while Mark packed soil around it to keep it steady.

Becky's thoughts drifted to the family in the photo. She wanted to learn more about them and the Bible they had just unearthed.

Chapter Twelve

"But whoever drinks the water I give them will never thirst." John 4:14

I⟶ HAD BEEN A few days since Mrs. Melody came to drop off the pie. Becky wanted to return the beautiful container the pie was in.

"Mark, maybe I should just drive the container over to Mrs. Melody." Becky hoped Mark would agree.

"Head down to the river like Mrs. Melody told us. It should lead you right to her house," Mark said as he grabbed a fishing rod. "I was going to the river to fish anyway, so I'll walk you down there."

Becky didn't know if Mark had already planned to go fishing or if he just wanted an excuse to accompany her down to the river. Even though there had been little romance between them in recent years, Mark always looked out for Becky. It had been that way since they were friends in college. That hadn't changed.

Mark settled in to fish when they reached the river, and Becky began her walk to Mrs. Melody's house.

After a few minutes of walking, the rushing river soothed Becky's anxious thoughts. It was a crisp morning but warmer than usual. There were so many birds out. Becky delighted in hearing them sing in the trees. She heard many unique sounds, and every once in a while, she caught a glimpse of a bird fluttering from branch to branch.

Just as the river was about to bend, Becky saw smoke in the sky. As she got closer, she noticed several chimneys with smoke billowing out. Through the trees, she could see a house; it looked stately yet cozy. *That must be Mrs. Melody's bed and breakfast*, she thought as she took in the vast land all around. *How does she take care of all that?*

Becky came to an arbor covered in climbing roses. She pushed open the small wooden gate. It led down a long and winding path through beautiful gardens. *Wow, this is amazing!*

It was quiet except for the crunching of gravel under Becky's boots. She came upon a fountain right in the middle of the path. As she went around it, she was captivated by the garden she stepped into. All the others were beautiful, but this one was distinctly stunning. It was bursting with roses of all colors. In the middle of the impressive array of roses was a statue of a little girl with arms outstretched, holding a dove. It was bronze, and the statue's workmanship was exceptional. Becky could see every detail of the girl's face. The inscription on the bottom of the statue read *In Loving Memory of Emma Rose, 1965–1975*.

Becky remembered the photo of the family in the buried box. *Could this be the same little girl in that photo?*

Just then, Becky heard someone singing. As she got closer, she could make out Mrs. Melody's deep, rich voice.

"Nobody knows the trouble I've seen
Nobody knows but Jesus."

There was such passion and soul in her voice. The tone was initially solemn, but then it became upbeat and joyful.

"Sometimes I'm up
Sometimes I'm down
Oh yes, my Lord."

As Becky walked closer, she saw Mrs. Melody on her knees, pulling weeds from the garden. Becky wanted to call out, but she didn't want to startle Mrs. Melody, who kept singing. A peace washed over Becky as she listened to the song's words, and the conviction in Mrs. Melody's voice gave her chills.

When Mrs. Melody finished singing, Becky called out gently so as not to alarm her. "Excuse me, Mrs. Melody . . ."

Mrs. Melody didn't startle; there wasn't much that could rattle her. "Come on over here, honey," she called to Becky. "I come out here often to pull weeds, or else they will take over the gardens." Mrs. Melody wiped the sweat from her brow.

"I heard you singing, Mrs. Melody. You have a beautiful voice."

"Aw, thank you, honey." Mrs. Melody looked up from underneath her large straw hat. She had kind eyes. They were the color of caramel.

Becky knelt down and began to help Mrs. Melody pull weeds. "I passed a garden on the way over, and there was a statue of a little girl—"

Mrs. Melody didn't let Becky finish the sentence. She began talking about her prized purple passionflowers. Mrs. Melody was a very polite Southern woman who would never interrupt another person who was speaking unless she was trying to change the subject. It was clear to Becky that Mrs. Melody didn't want to discuss the statue or the little girl.

Taking the hint, Becky commented about the purple passionflowers and continued the conversation. "Who helps you take care of all these gardens?"

"My husband helped me up until he passed away five years ago. After Emmett passed, our grandnephew, Martin, moved in to help care for the gardens and run the bed and breakfast. He's a fine young man." Mrs. Melody smiled with pride.

"I'm so sorry. How long were you married?"

"We had just celebrated sixty years of marriage before he passed."

"Sixty years; that's impressive! What's the secret to a good marriage?"

"It's all in how you prioritize your life. You put God first, your spouse second, and your children third, if you have kids. God wants to be first because He wants to help you in all those areas in your life."

Becky grew silent. Hearing what Mrs. Melody said struck her. Her life was not prioritized in that order at all. God was not first in her life. He was in the background, and she usually only called on Him in emergencies. It was also common for her to put work before her husband.

Becky was deep in thought until the rapid sound of gunfire jolted her. *Pop! Pop! Pop!*

Becky crouched as more shots were fired in the distance. Her heart was pounding so fast she could barely breathe. When she looked over at Mrs. Melody, she was not shaken.

Mrs. Melody placed her hand on Becky's shoulder. "It's okay, honey. Those are deer hunters. They're not coming after us."

As the two women stood up, they could hear loud thumping in the woods. They saw several deer leaping swiftly in between the trees. They were making their way over to the creek on Mrs. Melody's property.

"They know they're safe here."

Becky couldn't take her eyes off the deer, who were now just a few feet away from her. "I feel bad for them. They look so frightened."

The deer were panting. After a few minutes, once it seemed the threat had passed, the deer began to drink eagerly from the creek.

"Ah, as the deer pants for flowing streams, so pants my soul for you, O God." Mrs. Melody recited Psalm 42.

Becky looked at Mrs. Melody, puzzled by what the older woman said.

"Do you believe in God, Becky?"

"I was raised Christian, but I've drifted." Becky felt a tinge of embarrassment because it was clear that Mrs. Melody was a woman of faith.

"That's okay, honey. We all drift occasionally, but just like those deer, a soul thirsty for God will return to Him."

Becky couldn't remember the last time she thought of God; she couldn't even remember the last time she prayed.

Mrs. Melody noticed the sadness in Becky's eyes and gently reached out to take her hand in her own. "Becky," she said softly, "you are already deeply loved by God—more than you can ever imagine. We all are. The most important decision you'll ever make in your life is whether to love God in return."

Chapter Thirteen

"Set your minds on things above, not on earthly things." Colossians 3:2

A FEW MORNINGS EACH week, Katie called Becky to catch up. Becky loved hearing all about her daughter's college classes, her friends, and whatever else was happening with her. When Katie excitedly talked about her boyfriend, James, it brought back memories for Becky. Katie and James met in college, just like Becky and Mark had. Becky remembered those carefree days dating Mark: the late-night pizza runs, studying, and being silly together. It seemed like a lifetime ago.

As Becky was wrapping up her call with Katie, the doorbell rang. When Becky opened the door, she was surprised to find Mrs. Melody on her front porch, since it seemed her neighbor preferred the back route between the houses.

"I'm sorry I couldn't talk about Emma Rose's statue when you were over the other day," Mrs. Melody said, handing Becky a folder. "This should answer your questions."

Becky invited Mrs. Melody in, and they sat down on the couch. When Becky opened the folder, she came across a newspaper article.

Country Music Mogul's Wife and Daughter Die in Car Accident

Elizabeth Carter and her 10-year-old daughter, Emma Rose, were on their way to Nashville when a semitruck rammed into their car. Police say icy road conditions contributed to the fatal accident.

Becky looked up, saddened by what she read. "What about Joseph Carter? Where was he?"

"Elizabeth and Emma were on their way to see him in Nashville. Once Joseph hit it big in the music industry, he bought a big house in Nashville. Elizabeth and Emma Rose were going to join him there once she finished the school year here."

"Did you live next door when they lived in the cottage?"

"They were our best friends," Mrs. Melody said through tears. "My late husband, Emmett, and Joseph grew up together, and we were going to raise our kids together. I never could conceive a child; Emma Rose was like a daughter to me."

Becky offered Mrs. Melody some water and tissues.

After a few sips of water, Mrs. Melody continued. "You know that treasure everyone is always talkin' about? I can tell you what it is because Emmett and I were with Joseph when he buried it." Mrs. Melody paused for a few seconds. "After the accident, Joseph sold the mansion and returned to the cottage. He lived here until he died. He was seventy-five. He left all of his money to the children's home in Nashville. Money and fame didn't mean anything to him anymore. All that mattered to him was God and His word. That was his treasure. Joseph said he wished he had learned that earlier in life. It was God who got him through after he lost Elizabeth and Emma."

"Why bury the box? Why not leave it where it could be easily found?"

"The day he buried the box with his Bible, Joseph prayed over it. He believed that God would lead someone to find it. Someone who needed to be reminded of God's love for them."

Becky got up and came back, holding the box.

Mrs. Melody opened her eyes wide when she noticed Becky holding the box. She immediately recognized it because Joseph Carter's initials were etched on the front. She began to weep. "You found it!"

Becky held the box with the Bible in it close to her chest. She closed her eyes and began to cry. She had indeed found a treasure.

Chapter Fourteen

"Do not store up for yourselves treasures on earth, where moths and vermin destroy, and where thieves break in and steal." Matthew 6:19

EVER SINCE MRS. MELODY's visit, Becky began every morning reading the Bible that she found in Joseph Carter's box. She felt it was divine intervention that led her to it. She loved reading the notes Joseph had written in the margins of the tattered pages. The writings were heartfelt prayers and curious observations. It was clearly a well-loved Bible.

Some evenings, when Becky had a few minutes to herself, she read some passages. It was quite a departure from what Becky did back home to pass the time. For years, in the evenings, she would numb out by mindlessly scrolling on her phone or drink wine to try to relax from her stressful day.

Now she was hungry for something different. She was hungry to learn about God. Becky was raised in a family that attended church occasionally, but she had always been intimidated to read the Bible, apprehensive that she wouldn't understand it. A prayer Joseph Carter wrote in the margin encouraged her. He wrote:

Thank you, God, that your Word is alive and never returns void. Each day, I'm excited to see what you have in store for me. I trust that you will help me to understand what it is that I need to understand. Thank you for giving your son, Jesus, to die for my sins so I may have everlasting life with You. I love you with all of my heart and with all of my soul.

Becky's heart burst open when she read that. She wanted to fix her eyes on Jesus and let His Spirit lead her. The more she read and prayed, the more she began to feel herself being transformed. She was able to discern God's voice better; that soft whisper in her soul gently leading her and comforting her.

As Becky was curled up on the couch reading one morning, Mark came to sit next to her. "We need to talk."

Becky sat up; the tone in Mark's voice worried her.

"They made an arrest. They know who started the fire in our house." Mark took a deep breath before continuing. "It was Mateo."

Becky felt sucker punched hearing Mateo's name. "No, not Mateo! It can't be!" She grabbed her forehead and closed her eyes in disbelief.

Mateo had been friends with their son since second grade. He practically lived in their house while his parents were going through a bitter divorce. Mateo was like a son to them.

"I don't understand!" Becky exclaimed. "Maybe the investigators made a mistake."

"Mateo confessed. He never meant to burn the house. He tried to break into the safe with a blowtorch. The clothes in the closet caught fire and it spread to the bedroom. He panicked and ran out."

Becky had no words. She could never have imagined that the sweet boy she watched grow up, the boy who spent countless sleepovers at her house, would want to steal from them. She knew Mateo had been battling a drug addiction in recent months. She wondered if that's what led him to steal. It broke her heart.

"There's something else I need to tell you," Mark continued. "Jake is coming to visit on Monday. He's attending a medical conference in Nashville, and he wants to swing by to check on the progress we've made on his property."

Just when things couldn't get any worse, they did. Becky felt sick, knowing she would have to see Jake in a few days after decades of avoiding him.

Chapter Fifteen

"Be kind and compassionate to one another, forgiving each other, just as Christ God forgave you." Ephesians 4:32

IT WAS LATE SPRING, and the vegetable plants that Mark and Becky initially grew in the greenhouse and later planted in the ground were thriving. The garden was the one thing that brought them together nearly every day. Whether weeding and pruning or just talking about the plants that were growing, the garden seemed to be bearing fruit in their relationship.

Becky and Mark enjoyed sharing their harvest. Each week, they delivered fresh vegetables to Mrs. Melody for her bed and breakfast, and they donated the rest to a local food pantry run by the church Mrs. Melody attended. After working with the church's food pantry for several weeks, Becky and Mark began to attend service there.

Back at home they had attended church regularly when the kids were little but stopped when Katie and Josh became teenagers. Weekends were often consumed with traveling for soccer tournaments and dance competitions. Usually, Becky and Mark had to split up. Mark went with Josh, and Becky went with Katie. The family fell out of the rhythm of regularly attending church or doing much of anything outside of the kids' activities.

Being back at church felt good for Becky and Mark. They hadn't realized how spiritually hungry they were. Each week, they felt nourished by the worship and encouraged by the sermons and the community they found there. They began to look forward to Sundays.

One Sunday after church service, Mark surprised Becky with two bicycles he borrowed from Hank and Hilda from the general store. Mark wanted to help take Becky's mind off of Jake's upcoming visit.

"Let's take these down to the lake on Myrtle Street. We've been working so hard at the cottage. Let's have fun today!"

Becky looked at herself. "Mark, we're dressed in church clothes. Don't you think we're a little overdressed to be riding bikes?"

"It's beautiful out!" Mark rolled up the sleeves of his white shirt, loosened the collar, took his tie off, and shoved it into his pocket as he hopped on the bike. "Are you coming with me?"

Becky smiled. She grabbed the bottom of her floral maxi dress, bunched it up, knotted it, and hopped on the bike. "Let's go!" she said, laughing.

Becky and Mark meandered through the narrow roads between the charming historic buildings until they made it out of the village center and onto an open road. Wildflowers were blooming everywhere. A sea of pink, purple, and yellow covered the fields. Becky felt like a kid, so free riding on this country road. She felt alive and everything around her seemed more vibrant. The sky seemed bluer than she had ever seen it. The trees appeared greener.

She noticed Mark turn onto a side road, so she followed. In the distance, she could see the lake at the bottom. She stopped pedaling and let the downward slope of the road take her for a ride. She relaxed and took in the scenery while the cool breeze brushed against her face.

When Mark reached the lake's edge, he jumped off the bike, quickly unbuttoned his shirt, threw it on the sand, and ran toward the water.

"What are you doing?" Becky called out. "Isn't it cold?"

Mark threw himself in the water. He came up. "No, it's not too cold! Come on in, Beck!"

Mark hadn't called her Beck in so long. "You're crazy going in that water!" she shouted.

"I prefer charming!" Mark gave Becky an endearing smile.

Becky laughed. She stood on the lake's edge for a few minutes, watching Mark enjoy the water. He looked so happy!

She thought, *Why not join him?* She picked up the side of her dress and ran toward the water.

Mark was elated to see Becky coming. He held his hands out to her.

When she got to Mark, she grabbed his hands and tipped her head back into the water. When she came up, Mark gently brushed the wet hair away from her eyes. She smiled and looked into his eyes. For the first time in a long time, she could see Mark. The man she fell in love with.

"You know, I never stopped praying for us, for our marriage," Mark said. "All these years, I've held out hope and I never stopped loving you."

"Mark, I'm sorry for not making our marriage a priority. I was always so focused on work. When we started to have problems, instead of focusing on our marriage, I poured myself into work even more. I hope you can forgive me." Becky felt a weight lifted off of herself just saying those words.

"Of course I forgive you." Mark held Becky's hand. "I'm sorry I never told you how hurt I was. I just stopped trying to make our marriage work, and I let resentment build."

The two held each other in the lake and cried. The wall that had stood between them for years began to wash away. Although the road to healing their marriage was long, forgiveness helped pave the way.

Chapter Sixteen

"Now the serpent was more crafty than any
of the wild animals the Lord God had made."
Genesis 3:1

WHEN MONDAY MORNING ROLLED around, Becky and Mark had barely picked up from breakfast when they heard a car pull up on the gravel driveway. They were expecting Jake, but not this early.

It had been decades since Becky and Mark had seen Jake. As they peered out the window, they saw nothing had changed. Jake was still flashy. He stepped out of a metallic red Mercedes convertible. He hadn't lost his confidence or swagger. At six feet two, he thought of himself as a male model. He dressed and carried himself like one, but Jake was not a model; he was the head of a prominent plastic surgery practice in Miami, catering to the rich and famous.

He adjusted his aviator sunglasses as he walked toward the cottage, and he swept his dirty blonde hair away from his forehead.

Becky closed her eyes. Seeing Jake flooded her with so many terrible memories.

"Hi, Jake. Come on in," Mark said as he opened the door. "We're looking forward to showing you what we've done to the cottage." Mark was trying to keep things professional.

"Buddy, what's up?" Jake reached to shake Mark's hand while pulling him in for a hug. "It's been so long, man!"

"Yeah, it has. Come, let me show you what we've done." Mark spoke in a tone not matching Jake's enthusiasm. Mark just wanted to get the visit over with.

"Wow, the place looks amazing! Becky, you're so talented. I can see your touches all over."

Becky smiled stiffly. She hadn't realized just how much resentment she still carried toward Jake. *How can he walk around here aloof? Look at him! So suave. It's been twenty-eight years since he shattered my heart, and never once did he apologize.*

As Mark continued to share the details of what they had done to the cottage, Becky excused herself. "I'm so sorry, but I have to tend to something in the yard. I'll catch up with you later."

Becky didn't have to tend to anything; she needed fresh air. She began walking to the garden, talking to God. She could hear her wise friend Mrs. Melody's words echoing in her mind. *Cast all your burdens on God. He will take care of you.*

On this day, Becky had an earful to share with God. *God, I'm filled with rage right now! Why would you put me in a situation where I would have to face Jake again? I just want to forget I ever loved him. Help me, Father.*

Just as she finished the prayer, she saw Jake approaching.

"Wow, this garden is pretty cool!"

"Where is Mark?" Becky asked nervously.

"His boss called; it seemed urgent, so he had to take it."

All Becky could think to do was talk to Jake about the garden. Hopefully, he would leave soon. As Becky walked toward the garden, Jake followed closely behind her.

"The soil is great out here; we have—"

Before Becky could finish the sentence, Jake put his hand on her arm. Becky turned toward him. She was stunned.

"Becky, I didn't come here to see the cottage." Jake took off his sunglasses. "I came here to see you."

Becky looked away.

"I know it's been a long time, but I never stopped thinking about you. Come with me; we can be together like we were supposed to."

"You left me three days before our wedding. Are you serious, Jake? You couldn't even tell me yourself; you sent Mark to tell me!"

"Yeah, what a great friend he was! He ended up marrying you two years later."

"He was my friend too, Jake. You left everything in a million shattered pieces. Mark was there to pick up the mess you left behind. Do you know that I cried myself to sleep every night for weeks? I was saving myself for you, and you ended it all for a girl you met at a bar three weeks before we were supposed to get married! Do you know the sacrifice my parents made to pay for that wedding? They scraped every penny they had, and they couldn't get their money back."

"Well, I'm sure they were happy you married Mark, a fellow *Cubano*," Jake said smugly, stressing each syllable of the word *Cubano*.

"Oh my gosh, Jake! You just don't get it!"

"Listen, I can clearly provide for you much better than Mark can. Look, you're both living on my property. Marry me. I'll give you all the luxuries you've ever wanted."

"So you're asking me to be your wife?" Becky laughed at the nerve of Jake prancing into her life after twenty-eight years, with no apology, thinking he could just sweep her off her feet. "I would be your . . . third wife? Oh wait, I think I heard your last wife was number four. Please leave. You know what? Never mind. I'm leaving."

Jake grabbed Becky's arm firmly. "You're making a mistake."

Becky jerked her arm out of Jake's grip and looked straight into his eyes. "Mark is a better man than you'll ever be. God spared me from marrying you."

Just then, Mark approached. "What's going on?"

"I took care of it. I'll tell you later," Becky said.

Jake stormed by, got in his car, and sped away.

Chapter Seventeen

"Be joyful in hope, patient in affliction, and faithful in prayer." Romans 12:12

THAT AFTERNOON, MRS. MELODY came by for a visit, and the timing was perfect. Becky was still shaken up by Jake's visit. She needed sweet tea and soul talk with her cherished friend.

"Are you okay, honey?" Mrs. Melody took a seat next to Becky on the porch.

Becky told Mrs. Melody everything that happened with Jake.

"Mm mm, that Jake sounds like a real piece of work. Glad you sent him on his way."

"I don't think I realized how much resentment I had been carrying around. I'm glad I got to tell Jake how I felt. I'm exhausted, but I feel lighter." Becky sighed as she rested her head on the back of the rocking chair.

"Well, sometimes we don't know the extent of the pain we carry, but He knows." Mrs. Melody pointed to the sky.

"He sure does. Oh, I've been meaning to tell you that things with Mark are better."

Becky was grateful to have Mrs. Melody nearby. She helped her grow spiritually and gave her marriage advice too. Becky had opened up about the problems in her marriage a few months earlier.

"Like I always say, if you put God first, everything else will fall into place. I'm not saying it will always be easy, but it will be worth it. You have God's promise that He'll be with you through it all. The ups and downs."

"Mark and I have been spending a lot of time together, and we're enjoying each other's company, but it's been a long time since we were . . . intimate." Becky was hesitant to share.

"God designed physical intimacy between husband and wife as a sacred and beautiful gift, so there's no shame in it. You know my answer for everything is—"

"Pray," Mrs. Melody and Becky said together at the same time. They laughed.

"Yes, before you're intimate with your husband, pray. Pray over the two of you."

"Pray with him?" asked Becky.

"No, you can just pray silently in your head. It would make things less awkward."

They each took a sip of their sweet tea, paused, looked at each other, and laughed.

Chapter Eighteen

"That is why a man leaves his father and mother and is united to his wife, and they become one flesh." Genesis 2:24

THE NEXT DAY, BECKY planned a picnic for her and Mark in the yard under a canopy of oak trees. She brought out a big quilt, set everything up, and called Mark out.

"Oh wow, this looks amazing!" Mark was surprised by Becky's spontaneous invitation and the picnic lunch.

"Come, sit. I don't want the sandwiches to get soggy."

"Wait, are those wild berries growing in that bush?" Mark diverted his attention.

"Don't even think about eating one," Becky warned. "They could be poisonous."

Mark pulled a few off the bush and popped them into his mouth. "Mm . . . so good! You want some?"

"No, thank you. Our kids need at least one living parent."

The two chuckled and caught each other up on their morning. A few minutes later, Mark grabbed his throat and his eyes opened wide. "I feel my throat closing up," he muttered.

Becky fumbled to grab her phone in a panic. "I'm going to call 911!"

Mark struggled to breathe, and then suddenly he started to laugh. "I'm kidding! I'm kidding!"

Becky slapped his arm. "You're going to kill me one day with these practical jokes."

"I'm sorry. I couldn't help it." Mark chuckled as he laid down on the quilt.

Becky laid down next to him, looked up at the sky, and tried to relax so her racing heart could slow down.

Once she calmed down, she started to laugh. "You're ridiculous," she said, turning her head toward Mark.

"Ridiculously in love with you." Mark reached out to hold Becky's hand. "From the moment I saw you, I fell in love with you. I hated Jake for what he did to you, but I always knew you were too good for him."

Becky paused to process what Mark said. In twenty-six years of marriage, Mark had never mentioned Jake.

"I couldn't see it then, Mark, but I'm glad Jake ended our engagement. God turned the pain that Jake caused into something beautiful with you. Like that Bible verse says, 'God gives beauty for ashes.' "

Mark gently pulled Becky toward him. With tenderness, he lifted her chin and kissed her. Becky moved in closer. They began to kiss slowly and then more passionately. Mark's hands fell into the familiar crevices of his wife's body. The warmth of his touch made her feel secure and cherished.

"You're so beautiful," Mark said as he ran his fingers through Becky's hair.

Mark always saw beauty in Becky, even when she didn't see it herself. Becky wanted to be intimate with Mark, but she was nervous because it had been so long. She prayed silently. *God, be with us. Help us with our intimacy the way you designed it.*

Passion began to rise between them. Becky had forgotten how good it felt to feel Mark's body pressed against hers. Her heart raced and her skin was flushed from the excitement. They gave themselves to each other completely that afternoon. The connection they felt physically and emotionally was palpable.

Chapter Nineteen

"The rain came down, the streams rose, and the winds blew and beat against the house; yet it did not fall, because it had its foundation on the rock." Matthew 7:25

THE DAY MARK AND Becky had anticipated for months finally arrived. Their kids were coming to the cottage to spend the summer with them. As they hurried to prepare for their visit, they noticed the forecast included severe thunderstorms headed their way.

"I hope this weather doesn't affect their flight," Becky said.

"They should land before the worst of it gets here," Mark said as he looked at the forecast on his phone. Mark and Becky had to drive about thirty minutes to pick Katie and Josh up at the airport in Nashville.

When they got to the airport, they both scanned the crowd of people on the curb. Becky immediately spotted Josh with his guitar slung over his shoulder. He never went anywhere without it. Right next to him was Katie. Her hair was slicked back in a high ponytail, and AirPods were tucked in her ears.

"Pull in here!" Becky excitedly motioned to Mark.

The moment the car stopped, Becky jumped out and ran over to the kids. She gave each a big hug. "I'm so happy you're here!"

Mark got out of the car. He gave Katie and Josh a hug, then quickly loaded the suitcases in the trunk. They needed to rush because the weather had intensified and the area was under a tornado watch.

Mark, Becky, and the kids arrived safely at the cottage and tucked themselves in. All night, the cottage was pelted with rain and occasional hail. The wind gusts were tossing things around outside in all directions. It was an intense storm, but the kids were so exhausted from traveling that they slept the whole night unbothered. Mark and Becky slept well too. They were happy to have their children under one roof. It had been a long time since they were all together.

Chapter Twenty

"Are not two sparrows sold for a penny? Yet not one of them will fall to the ground outside your Father's care." Matthew 10:29

THE NEXT DAY, THE sun gave way to a beautiful morning. It was hard to believe the night had been so tumultuous. While the kids were still sleeping, Mark and Becky went out to assess the storm damage. There was no damage to the cottage. There were just downed tree limbs scattered all around.

Among a pile of tree limbs, Mark noticed something moving. As he got closer, he could see it was a baby bird. It was so young it had no feathers and could barely lift its head. Mark looked around for a nest to put the bird back in, but he couldn't find one.

Becky noticed the bird. "Oh . . . that poor baby. If we can't find a nest, we'll have to care for her."

"Let's leave her here for a bit and see if her mom comes around," Mark suggested.

Becky and Mark went inside and waited by the window. After about an hour, Becky began to grow impatient. She could see the helpless bird trying to move with little strength.

Becky filled a basket with shredded leaves to create a makeshift nest. "I'm going to bring her inside. We've been watching for some time, and no mama bird has come for her. An animal could eat her. I'm not waiting any longer."

After bringing the bird in and getting her warm, Becky made a food mixture she had read about on a wildlife rescue website. "This little girl is so hungry!"

Mark watched the bird devour the food. "I read that at the beginning, baby birds must be fed every half-hour, so we'll all have our hands full. We'll have to take turns caring for her. Even the kids will have to pitch in."

Chapter Twenty-one

"I came that they may have life and have it abundantly." John 10:10

For weeks, the baby bird they named Esperanza, which means hope in Spanish, took up much of the Ruiz's time. Becky and Mark took turns feeding at night. Katie and Josh handled the day feedings. It was a lot of work, but it was worth it. In the beginning, Esperanza was so weak they didn't know if she would make it through those first few days, but she turned the corner. Each day, she grew stronger.

"Mom, how will we know when Esperanza will be ready to be released?" Josh asked.

"Her wings seem strong and she's been eating on her own, so I think soon."

Katie walked in on the conversation. "I'm going to miss her, and I'm going to miss this cottage. It's not home, but it felt good being here this summer."

Becky understood exactly what Katie was feeling. She felt peace and joy there too. It was where she grew in her relationship with God and her marriage began to heal. Becky wanted to stay in the cottage longer, but Jake had a buyer and they needed to leave.

The Ruiz family didn't know where they would go next. Their home was still not ready. Despite the uncertainty, Becky had an innate peace that it would be okay. The peace, joy, and healing didn't come from the cottage or the land. They came from God, and He would be with her wherever she went.

"Esperanza will be okay, and so will we," Becky assured Katie and Josh.

Becky remembered something that Joseph Carter wrote in the margin of Genesis in his Bible.

Deep within every human heart lies a longing for Eden. An innate desire to be loved and to be in the presence of our Creator, like it was in the Garden, where it all began. We try to create "our own Eden" with things that promise to bring us delight, but nothing in this world can truly satisfy, because we were made for more. Our purpose is simply to know God and to make him known.

Chapter Twenty-two

"Those who hope in the Lord will renew their strength. They will soar on wings like eagles."
Isaiah 40:31

THE DAY ARRIVED WHEN Esperanza was ready to be released. Josh brought the cage over and placed it under a large oak tree. It was a bittersweet day for the Ruiz family. Caring for the little bird around the clock for weeks brought them together as a family in a way they hadn't been in a long time. They were grateful their efforts paid off and she was ready to go, but it was hard to say goodbye.

"I think we should pray before we let her out," Katie suggested.

"That's a good idea." Becky reached one hand out to Mark and the other to Mrs. Melody, who was at her other side.

Becky, Mark, Mrs. Melody, Josh, and Katie held hands to form a circle around the cage. They bowed their heads and Mark prayed.

"Lord, thank you. We had hoped and prayed for this day when Esperanza would be strong enough to fly. We ask that you watch over our little feathered friend and watch over us as we leave this cottage to start a new chapter in our lives. We thank you for our family and for friends who became family. In Jesus's name, we pray. Amen."

"Is everyone ready?" Mark asked, placing his hand on the cage's door.

Becky nodded and Mark opened the door. They imagined that Esperanza would immediately fly out, but she didn't. She stayed in the cage. All the anticipation they had built up was quickly flattened.

Katie knelt close to the cage and whispered, "It's okay, girl. It's safe. You can go."

Suddenly Esperanza flew out and landed on the grass just a few feet away. She pumped her wings several times but landed in the same spot on the ground. She was struggling to take flight.

"What if we let Esperanza go too early? Maybe we should have kept her with us longer." Josh sounded panicked.

Becky, who would normally have been the one to worry, was not fearful. She had faith and therefore hope. "Esperanza will be fine. God brought her this far, and He won't fail her now."

Mrs. Melody looked at Becky and smiled. She knew Becky wasn't just talking about the bird.

Esperanza pumped her wings again, and within seconds, she took flight. She kept flying higher and further. She soared so far that eventually they lost sight of her.

Becky took a deep breath and exhaled. Tears welled up in her eyes. "Even if trouble comes, she'll be okay. She now knows the way. She's free. She's finally free."

**Jesus said, "I am the way and
the truth and the life." John 14:6**

Reflection Questions

1. The word Eden means "delight." In what ways do you think you attempt to "create your own Eden" with worldly things? For example: obtaining material things, status/followers, seeking control and/or perfection, keeping up with pretenses, or in other ways. What has it cost you?

2. "For God so loved the world, that he gave his only Son, that whoever believes in Him should not perish but have eternal life." John 3:16 What does this verse mean to you?

3. "Create in me a clean heart, O God, and renew a right spirit within me." Psalm 51:10 Ask God to search your heart. What are some things you want to confess? Is there anyone you need to forgive?

4. "Looking to Jesus, the founder and perfecter of our faith." Hebrews 12:2 What are some things/situations that you are holding onto that you feel you could surrender to God?

5. Spend a few minutes in prayer and jot down whatever stirs in your heart.

About the Author

Jaylene Rodriguez-Garau, a first-generation American and daughter of Cuban parents, brings a unique perspective to her writing. A former NBC reporter, she combines her journalistic experience with her faith, to create meaningful and impactful short stories. When she's not writing, Jaylene enjoys spending time with her husband and daughter. She writes fiction with purpose to encourage others to know God and to make Him known.

www.jaylenerodriguezgarau.com

www.ingramcontent.com/pod-product-compliance
Lightning Source LLC
Chambersburg PA
CBHW020312150626
46552CB00022B/2852